Lucia,
Happy Bi
8/13/20

Lucia,
Love You,
Zia Domenica
Zio Richie

Donation
Here!!

Dear Parents,

Lucy to the Rescue is based on a true story—the story of my own rescued dogs.

Lucy was my first rescued dog. After rescuing and adopting our second rescued dog, Lily, who had just been diagnosed with mammary carcinosarcoma, I was inspired to start the nonprofit organization Lucy the Rescue Dog, Inc.

I wrote this story to be the voice of the millions of dogs (and cats) living in shelters across the country. Many of the animals are euthanized because of overcrowding. Lucy and Lily were both in high-kill shelters and on death row. It's my hope that after reading this book, you will adopt a dog or cat from a shelter or rescue organization and give them a forever home, too.

I hope you enjoy reading *Lucy to the Rescue* as much as I enjoyed writing it—and as much as I enjoy my own real-life rescued dogs.

To my husband, Joe: Thank you for motivating me and encouraging me to write and share our story.

To Allison Bell, Sonja Ender Reinert, Lesley Chadwick, and Diana Madison Colello from Perfect Pets Rescue, Inc.: Thank you for saving Lucy's life. Thanks to Lucy's foster mom in New York, Kim Kleine, for helping Lucy find her forever home with us. We are forever grateful.

To Gayla Adams Hurwitz from FurBaby Rescue, Inc.: Thank you for saving Lily's life. Thanks to Lily's foster mom in North Carolina, Holly Dormeyer, for taking Lily for surgery and helping her find her forever home with us.

www.mascotbooks.com

Lucy to the Rescue

For more information, please contact:
Mascot Books
620 Herndon Parkway, Suite 320
Herndon, VA 20170
info@mascotbooks.com

Library of Congress Control Number: 2020902768

CPSIA Code: PRT0520A
ISBN-13: 978-1-64543-453-5

Printed in the United States

LUCY TO THE RESCUE

DEBORAH PORCO

ILLUSTRATED BY JUAN DIAZ

Animal Shelter
LUCY

Hi, my name is Lucy. I was rescued from an animal shelter in Atlanta, Georgia and given a second chance at life.

Animal Shelter

A rescue organization brought me to New York, and I waited for a family to adopt me. Every night when I went to sleep, I wished for a home and a family to call my own.

One day my foster mom told me that there were some people coming to see me.

I was hoping that would be my lucky day. It was! I ran up to the man and licked him on the cheek when he knelt down to pet me. It was love at first sight. I was adopted, and now I have a family.

I moved into a farmhouse, and I have a fenced-in yard to run and play. I am loved and a very happy dog.

My mommy and daddy even let me sit on the couch and sleep on the bed at night. I've gone to puppy school and graduated, and now I'm a Canine Good Citizen. That means I'm a good dog and I mind my manners.

Mommy says, "Dogs are family," and she wants to help pets that are sick or injured and need veterinary care when families can't afford treatment.
Dogs are family

Mommy said, "Lucy, there is a dog in North Carolina who is sick. We should go help her." So we got in the car and drove to North Carolina to meet Lily the Chihuahua.

Lily was sick and
needed a home, so
we adopted her and
brought her home with
us to New York.

Lily was so grateful to be adopted,
and we bonded immediately. We became
inseparable, napping and snuggling together, and
became best friends.

We were so happy to be able to give Lily a home. I wished we could help more sick pets. Then, Mommy had an idea.

Lucy
the Rescue Dog
Charity

My mommy said, "Lucy, we could start a charity and call it *Lucy the Rescue Dog, Inc.*" We could help the families of sick or injured pets when their parents cannot do it alone.

My daddy said, "We can have fundraisers on our farm and raise money to help the sick or injured pets." Mommy agreed that this was a great idea.

Donation
Here !!

Mommy and Daddy invited their friends to a birthday party for me, and all the guests donated money to help the sick or injured pets. The best thing about the party was that some people even brought their dogs! I made so many new friends! Even the rescue organization that rescued me brought dogs and cats from their shelters to get adopted, too. It was just like my adoption day all over again, and I was so excited that my family was helping other animals find homes and raising money to help other animals.

Mommy says "Lucy to the Rescue" when a veterinarian calls and asks if Lucy can help a family in need. She says, "Lucy, you are doing a wonderful job, and so many families are grateful."

THE END

In loving memory of Joe Porco

About the Author

Deborah Porco is a first-time author and president and founder of Lucy the Rescue Dog Inc., a 501 (c)(3) nonprofit public charity. Her compassion and love for animals is her inspiration for her charity. She resides in New Paltz, New York with her rescued pets.